The Right Note

REALITY SHOW

The Right Note

D. A. GRAHAM

MINNEAPOLIS

Darby Creek
A division of Lerner Publishing Group, Inc.
241 First Avenue North
Minneapolis, MN 55401 USA

For reading levels and more information, look up this title at www.lernerbooks.com.

Cover: Moomusician/Shutterstock.com; wawritto/Shutterstock.com; Redshinestudio/Shutterstock.com.

Main body text set in Janson Text LT Std 12/17.5.
Typeface provided by Adobe Systems.

Library of Congress Cataloging-in-Publication Data

Names: Graham, D. A., 1995– author.
Title: The right note / by D.A. Graham.
Description: Minneapolis : Darby Creek, [2019] | Series: Reality show | Summary: Music duo Eve and Ryan are ecstatic to be contestants on their favorite show, The Right Note, but when the producers decide they should perform as solo acts, the duo's ambition and friendship are put to the test.
Identifiers: LCCN 2018014397 (print) | LCCN 2018020309 (ebook) | ISBN 9781541541887 (eb pdf) | ISBN 9781541540255 (lb : alk. paper) | ISBN 9781541545441 (pb : alk. paper)
Subjects: | CYAC: Reality television programs—Fiction. | Singing—Fiction. | Friendship—Fiction.
Classification: LCC PZ7.1.G716 (ebook) | LCC PZ7.1.G716 Ri 2019 (print) | DDC [Fic]—dc23

LC record available at https://lccn.loc.gov/2018014397

Manufactured in the United States of America
1-45230-36612-8/13/2018

CHAPTER 1

On the way to the audition, I turn to Ryan and whisper, "Are you ready to rock?" He gives me a nervous smile at my joke—we aren't a *rock* band—but he doesn't say anything. I wipe my sweaty hands on my jeans. Apparently neither of us is ready to rock.

We're on the bus headed downtown to audition for our favorite TV show: *The Right Note*. It's a music competition, where musicians from all over the country sing and dance their way to the top. Each season has a different theme, and this time around the theme is "teamwork." For this season, only music duos are allowed to audition. Eight duos from all over the country will compete over the course of a month for an awesome grand prize: a record deal with Wild Hill Studio, the company that created the show. Only one person can win, but they can choose their duo partner or another competitor to join the record deal. If either Ryan or I win the competition, the two of us will get to record an album.

When the announcement came out that *The Right Note* would be holding auditions in our hometown, Ryan convinced me to sign up with him, claiming it would be the perfect opportunity for us.

It's true that being on the show would be huge for me and Ryan. We've been a music duo ever since we were in the same after-school guitar class as kids. Even though we're both talented, it's hard to get noticed. All of our performances have been at my mom's café, with audiences of maybe a dozen people.

Until now, that is. Millions of people watch *The Right Note* each season. The winner of the first season, Cassandra Holmes, sold half a million albums in a week. The thought of performing on reality TV terrifies me, but I want to share our music with the world, and winning will give us the opportunity to do just that.

We aren't the only ones thinking about the prize and success. On the bus with us is a pair of girls our age covered in glitter. Behind them, a guy with a leather jacket and a violin sits next to his guitarist partner.

I'm wearing my lucky sweatshirt. Ryan, however, has decided to dye his hair blue for the occasion. How we should look was one of the things we argued about during our practices. Ryan wanted us to stand out and be colorful. I wanted us to impress the judges with our sound, not our looks. In the end, we decided to each dress how we wanted—which is good because I'd look bad with blue hair.

As the bus comes to a stop, I pick up my guitar case and tug on Ryan's sleeve. He follows me off the bus to the football stadium. The auditions are inside one of the event rooms here. The stadium has never seemed so big before.

I grin to hide my nervousness. "Let's knock their socks off."

***

The stadium is packed full of musicians and their families and friends. Some of them are tuning their instruments, while others are practicing singing or talking in groups. All the noise blends into one harsh note. Out of the corner of my eye, I see Ryan turn on his sampler and record it for a few seconds.

The sampler is like a computer and a piano keyboard put together. During our practices, Ryan records different sounds and then twists a bunch of knobs on the sampler to transform the sounds into music. I don't know how he does it, but after his tinkering, it always sounds really cool.

My music is a bit more traditional. I play the guitar and sing almost all the vocals for our songs. My voice is very soft, and I like to contrast it with harsh guitar riffs inspired by rock and roll and heavy metal. When Ryan and I perform together and combine our different types of music, we sound like no one else. We aren't rock or electronica or pop but instead a combination of the three. That's why we're going to win *The Right Note*: we're totally unique.

Ryan and I settle down in the stadium seats near a pair of rowdy singers who are practicing their a cappella song. Both of them harmonize in a different key. It sounds horrible. They seem to think so, too, because one of them starts shouting at the other, and then the other shouts back. Ryan laughs to himself.

The a cappella duo finally pulls out a harmonica to get them in the same key. It still isn't very good, but at least they aren't arguing anymore. I spend the waiting period tuning and testing out my guitar, and Ryan messes around with the sample he took of the stadium.

After about half the stadium has been cleared out, Ryan and I get called into the audition room. There are four judges sitting at a table with a video camera planted in front of them. These aren't the famous judges who will appear on the show but instead local music lovers in charge of deciding who's good enough to go to the California studio. One of them, a grumpy-looking old man with a mustache, says, "Eve Hardt and Ryan Okri. Welcome to the auditions for *The Right Note*. What will you be doing for us today?"

I pluck my guitar out of its case as Ryan sets up the stand for the sampler. "We're going to perform a song we wrote," Ryan says. "It's called 'The Quiet Night.'"

This song is one of my favorites of ours. It's unlike all our others because we play it slightly differently every time. I always start with the same chords and sing the same lyrics, but then it's up to Ryan what to do with the sample. I play the guitar based on what the sample sounds like. We go back and forth, responding to each other with our music.

"Great. Ready when you are," says one of the judges.

"Good luck," adds another.

I meet Ryan's eyes. We nod at each other.

I start the song by strumming a sequence of chords on my guitar, which Ryan records into the sampler. He plays it back and then twists a couple of knobs to warp the sound. It turns into something eerie, like an alien's version of guitar. Meanwhile, I keep strumming those same chords. Then I pause, and Ryan turns the recording into a swirl of notes. When he stops playing the recording and silence falls over the room, I start singing.

After Ryan adds more layers of sound, he lets the volume drop, and this time he sings. He hits the notes along with the sampler, so his voice sounds digitized. I come in on the last word, and we sing the chorus together.

Ryan and I go all out, dancing to the electronic beat that fills the room. I let out a riff on the guitar. One of the judge's eyebrows shoot up, and the one on the other end of the table breaks out into a grin. Even the grumpy guy taps his foot under the table.

I finish off the song with its final verse. Our instruments sync together. After I sing the final word, I let out three loud chords from my guitar and the song ends.

Then the judges applaud.

"Not a very quiet night after all," the grumpy judge says. The others laugh. "What a great performance. You two have such wonderful energy."

"Thank you," Ryan and I say together, breathless.

"We'll be in touch about the results of the auditions in the next week. Expect a letter in the mail. Take care." The judge winks. "Next!"

CHAPTER

2

The letter comes the next Saturday. I rush
to the truck and snatch the mail when the
mailman arrives in the morning. Bill, bill,
Mom's fashion magazine, ad, bill, and then
there it is—a bright yellow envelope from
Wild Hill Studio. I drop the rest of the mail
to the sidewalk.

I flip the envelope over and stare at
the flap. Between me and this envelope is
my destiny.

Then I peel it back and pull the letter out.

The first word I see tells me everything
I need to know. I nearly drop this letter too.

A vibration like a music note fills my body from my toes to my head. I want to let out a scream, but my voice gets caught in my throat. I need to let this energy out somehow. So I decide to sprint to Ryan's house.

But as I'm about to round the corner, a blue smear slams into me and knocks me onto my back. The letter goes flying through the air.

"Ow!" a familiar voice cries.

I sit up. Ryan is flat on the sidewalk right in front of me, rubbing his forehead. Next to him is his own yellow envelope. Our letters flutter to the ground around us.

When Ryan sees that it's me who nearly ran him over, he breaks into a huge grin. "Eve—we did it!" he squeaks.

Finally I can speak again. I laugh as I help Ryan to his feet. We hold onto each other as we jump up and down, spinning and celebrating.

I scoop up my letter from the sidewalk, staring at that one word: "Congratulations!" And, folded into the letter, is a plane ticket to California scheduled for next week.

Over the next few days, I barely sleep. I spend as much time as possible practicing my guitar. I sing in the shower, pretending my shampoo bottle is a microphone. In my head, all I can hear are the excited crowds. All I can see are the spotlights. Our parents are also excited, but they can't afford to take a sudden vacation and come with us to California. It'll just be me and Ryan, which only excites me more. It feels like going on tour.

Then, finally, the day arrives. Ryan and I fly out to California. As soon as we land and grab our bags from the conveyer belt, a young woman comes bounding up to us. Her hair is so blond it is almost white, and she wears a wireless ear piece on her right ear.

"Eve Hardt! Ryan Okri!" she exclaims. She takes my hand and shakes it vigorously. Then Ryan's. "Hello, hello, hello! I'm Blair Casanova. I'm one of the production assistants of *The Right Note*. I'm here to pick you up and take you on a tour of the studio. Do you have all your things? Are you ready to go? I am so excited to finally meet you. I *loved* your audition. The way the two of you play off each other is exactly the kind of thing we're looking for. You are such *characters*!"

She speaks rapid-fire fast. Before Ryan and I can respond, she marches us out the doors of the airport.

"You two are going to love the studio. It has everything you could ever need: lights, camera, and action. And, of course, any instrument you can name. If we don't have it, we'll get it."

Ryan looks at me. "Whoa."

"Whoa is right. Trust me—after this, you two are never going to look at music the same way again." Blair bounces in her high heels as she walks. Her excitement is contagious. Ryan starts bouncing too. I can't help but laugh at the two of them as they bounce in sync.

We ride with Blair down the palm-tree-lined streets in a shiny black SUV that still smells brand new. The whole way, she chatters on and on, dumping a load of information on us. Overwhelmed, I tune her out. Beside me, Ryan leans in to Blair's every word, his face alight with curiosity and enthusiasm. They're practically friends already.

We arrive at the studio after an hour in the car. As soon as we get out of the SUV, a young man takes our bags and instruments off to the residence hall where all the contestants will stay. After he disappears, Blair takes us to the building where they film the performances. I've seen this building on TV a million times. It looks like a huge glass brick, the outside completely covered in windows. At night, it sparkles like a rainbow disco ball, with big lights shining out of all the windows.

Blair marches us down the halls of the studio. She shows us the dressing rooms, which are packed with designer clothes, makeup, and mirrors. Then the rehearsal rooms, where the vocal trainers will help us practice for each competition. Then the room where the film editors work, which is filled with TV screens and a table covered in buttons a lot like Ryan's sampler.

Finally, Blair leads me and Ryan through a pair of double doors, and suddenly we're inside the performance hall. It looks so much bigger and brighter in person. It's more like a cave than a theater, with a curved ceiling and lights hanging down. The floor slopes down from us to the stage. Huge curtains with gold tassels drape over the walls. Lights of every color flicker on and off randomly. The show's logo, a huge rainbow encircling the words "The Right Note" glows on the back wall. In the middle of the stage stands a man with his hands on his hips.

My jaw drops.

It's Tix. Ten years ago, Tix was one of the most popular musicians in America. Now he hosts *The Right Note*. On TV, he smiles wide, wears glittering suits, and puts an arm around each of the contestants as he introduces them. In a few days, his arm will be around me, and he'll be yelling my name to the cheering crowds. I begin to sweat a little even though the air conditioning is on full blast. My heart thuds. This is really happening.

Suddenly, a huge spotlight shines on Tix, lighting up his bald head. He throws his hands up to shield his eyes. "Hey! I said to turn on stage *left*, not center stage," he shouts angrily. "I always enter from stage left. Stage left, pause, I say my lines, you follow me to the center—"

The light shuts off. "Sorry, Mr. Tix," says the stagehand in charge of the spotlights, a pimply boy not much older than me and Ryan.

"For the millionth time, it's just Tix!" Tix rubs his temples. To himself, he grumbles, "No one ever listens to me."

"Tix!" Blair cries. She pulls me and Ryan down the sloped floor to the stage. "I'm so glad you're here. I want to introduce you to two more contestants: Eve Hardt and—"

"Yeah, yeah, I'll get their names when you give me the updated script, Blair." Tix waves a hand at her. His eyes pass over me and Ryan like we aren't even here. "Why aren't you working on that, by the way?"

Blair looks startled. For the first time, her huge smile disappears. "Well, I had to pick up these two from the airport, and I wanted to show them around—"

"Hold on a second," he cuts her off,

then glares at the nearest stagehand. "Can someone please hurry up with my coconut water?" The girl yelps and disappears behind the curtains. Tix turns back to us. His gray eyes finally meet mine, and I realize how old he looks. He scowls at us. No amount of coconut water can fix the meanness in his face. "And you, Blair. No more excuses. Get back to work."

Blair deflates. She nudges me to let me know it's time to go. But then Ryan blurts out, "Dude, what is your problem?"

Typical Ryan, not knowing when to stay quiet. A vein appears on Tix's forehead. I wince, waiting for him to yell in our direction next. But instead he asks, "What's your name, kid?"

"Ryan Okri."

"Let me give you some advice, Ryan Okri. The music industry isn't about being nice. It's about fighting for what you want." Tix gestures dramatically around him. "This whole thing, this whole show, is a fight. Don't be afraid to push everyone else to the sidelines, and don't stop to feel bad about it. In show business, you're the only person who matters." He jabbed a finger at Ryan. "Got it?"

Ryan furrows his brow. "Okay . . ."

Someone calls to Tix from offstage, and he hurries away from us as if he's already forgotten we're here. Blair escorts us from the performance hall. As soon as we leave, she goes back to normal, like the conversation with Tix never happened. But I feel a new weight hanging on my heart. Ryan trudges along beside me. One of our favorite musicians has turned out to be a washed-up jerk. I guess not everything is as seen on TV.

CHAPTER

3

Suddenly it's the first day of filming. I barely
get out of bed before Ryan barges in and yells
that we have to hurry down to the studio. He
reaches into my closet and throws a shirt at me.

The studio is even more of a whirlwind
of activity than yesterday. Camera crews and
stagehands rush around carrying equipment,
paperwork, and coconut waters. Out of the
fray comes Blair in her high heels and perfectly
sleek hair. "You two are late!" she scolds.
"Come on."

She drags us into the dressing room and
starts throwing clothes at us, just like Ryan

did to me only minutes ago. "Eve—put this on. We need to make sure the logo is showing while you're on camera. Ryan—try this." She fluffs and tugs and pats us down until she's decided we look presentable enough. Instead of my usual comfy sweatshirt, I'm wearing a stiff faux leather jacket. Ryan's new outfit consists of a bright red blazer and matching tie. With his blue hair, he looks like a parrot.

"What was wrong with our own clothes?" I whisper to Ryan.

"It's just part of the whole reality show thing," he replies. "We have to look like celebrities."

Maybe he's right, but I don't like it very much. Ryan doesn't seem bothered, though, so I try to push my discomfort aside.

Next, Blair opens a door on the other side of the dressing room and reveals what looks like a waiting room at a doctor's office. Except rather than being full of patients, it's full of teenage musicians. The other seven duos. Fourteen pairs of eyes stare at me and Ryan as we sit down. I flush, my nervousness returning.

All of them look like professional musicians. The ones who catch my eye are two punk girls with spiky black hair, a boy in a cowboy hat who flashes me a creepy smile, and a girl whose small mouth makes her look like she's constantly displeased.

Blair claps her hands together loudly, interrupting the stare down.

"Hello, contestants!" she says. "Welcome to the first episode of *The Right Note*! If you haven't already met me, I'm Blair Casanova, one of the production assistants. And I am so excited to be here with you all because this season's theme of 'teamwork' is really special! We're going to shine the spotlight on how you duos work together, compete with each other, and make friends—or enemies—with each other.

"For the first two weeks of the show, you're all going to compete on teams chosen and coached by the judges. In a moment, each duo will head to the stage to perform in front of the judges, and then they will decide what team to put you on. Isn't that exciting?"

Some of the contestants murmur in agreement.

Blair continues, "Every three days there will be an elimination round where all the teams perform. At the end of the round, the judges will choose which team did the worst and send home one of that team's members. So you'll want to work together with your teammates to put on a good show. When there are only ten of you remaining, we'll change things up a bit and have you all perform solo in front of the judges until we get to the final four contestants. Those final four will perform one last time, and from there the judges will choose the winner."

After a brief pause she continues, "I hope you're all ready to show the judges what you've got! But before I send anyone out there, we're going to film some quick introductions to each of the duos so our viewers can get to know you all. How does that sound?"

The boy with the cowboy hat says in a Southern accent, "Sounds good to me!"

"Fantastic!" Blair exclaims. "Do you and Lark want to go first, Asher?"

"Yeah, we do." The boy in the cowboy hat looks eagerly at the girl with the small mouth. She shrugs.

One by one, the duos vanish through the door. Ryan and I go last because we arrived late. When it's our turn, Blair takes us to a small orange room and sits us down on a pair of stools. Behind us is the rainbow logo of *The Right Note*. She goes behind one of the cameras. "Hello, my dears. Are you comfortable? Feeling excited? Ready to go?" Ryan and I make eye contact, clearly uncomfortable about being on camera for the first time. Blair continues without our response, "Great. I need you two to look at this camera when you answer your questions. Rolling in five."

I look up at Blair's hand, which holds up five fingers. Then four. Three. Two. One. A red light pops up on the side of the camera. We're recording.

The questions are all about what it's like being a duo together. How did we meet? What kind of music do we make? What are our inspirations? I tell the cameras about how

Ryan and I became friends almost instantly. We were the only kids in our guitar class who could successfully play "Twinkle, Twinkle, Little Star" by the end of the first lesson. Ryan talks about wanting to start a band with me because he thought I was really cool, even though everyone else thought I was a shy, quiet kid. Then I talk about our first live performance at the middle school talent show. And about how we watch every season of *The Right Note* together.

Then, Blair asks each of us what we admire most about each other.

"I love how you break the rules," I say to Ryan. "You make music out of everything. It's like your superpower."

"And I love how you keep it real," Ryan says to me. "You remind me not to go too crazy."

"How sweet," Blair coos as the cameras shut off. "Oh, that was so wonderful. I hope you're ready to go in front of the judges and show them what you've got. They're going to love you."

We follow her down the hall to the backstage area. Leaning against the wall are my guitar and Ryan's sampler. I rush over and grab the guitar. Its familiar curves feel so much like home that I instantly relax.

Then Tix's voice booms from the other side of the curtain, announcing our arrival: "Our final duo, Eve Hardt and Ryan Okri!" He sounds cheerful and proud—the opposite of when Ryan and I first met him.

We pick up our instruments and race onto the stage and into the spotlights.

My first glimpse is of the judges. They are sitting at their table, staring right at me. On the right is Xavier Sandalwood, one of the most famous songwriters in pop music. Next to him is Peter Vasquez, the harshest judge on reality TV. Then, Marina Murphy, an opera-singer-turned-pop-star from Ireland whose concerts bring in thousands of screaming fans. Finally, at the end is Cassandra Holmes, my idol and the winner of the first season of *The Right Note*. My heart nearly stops. These judges are the best of the best, the biggest names in music. The cameras, spotlights, and judges' eyes are all on us.

I gulp. But Ryan doesn't seem fazed by any of this. He sets up at his sampler and gestures for me to plug in my guitar. So I do. And before I know it we're jamming "The Quiet Night" again. Ryan goes all out with the layers of sound, bringing me out of my funk and into the music. I sing my heart out. I realize with the spotlights shining brightly into my eyes, I can't see anyone except the judges. No audience to stare me down. I even risk doing a little shimmy.

But then Ryan's voice cracks during his part. He closes his mouth and his face turns as red as his jacket. Thinking quickly, I fill the void with some freestyle guitar.

When we finish, the judges clap. Tix comes out from the darkness, also applauding us. "Bravo, bravo!" he cries. He claps Ryan on the back and shakes my shoulder. "What a performance from our last duo of the day! Let's see what the judges thought."

"I thought it was splendid. Just great. You wrote that yourselves?" Xavier asks.

Marina nods. "Brilliant. Absolutely brilliant."

"I agree. Some iffy vocals from that one, but nothing we can't work with," says Peter, pointing his pen at Ryan.

"The way you two perform is . . . very interesting," says Cassandra.

I cross my fingers behind my back that Cassandra picks us. She knows what it's like to come from the bottom and rise to the top.

The judges whisper to each other for a few seconds.

Then, Cassandra looks at me. "I will take Eve."

My heart soars and I break into a huge grin.

"And I want Ryan." Peter points at him with the pen again.

My face falls. "Wait, what? You're putting us on two different teams?"

"That's right."

"We're a duo," Ryan says. "You can't split us up."

"You aren't the only duo we've split up," says Xavier.

"As the judges, we get to pick the teams," Peter says.

Cassandra leans back in her chair. "You two are a remarkable pair. But we want to push each of you to be the best musicians you can be. We believe that can only happen if you compete *against* each other." She points at Ryan. "He needs some work on his voice. That's why he's going on Peter's team. And you, Eve, need to embrace the *passion* of the music. That's why I want you."

"But we came here together. We want to go on to record an album together," I protest.

"I can't compete *against* Eve," Ryan says.

Peter glowers at us. "If you can't compete against her, then you're welcome to drop out of the competition. There are plenty of other duos out there who would love to fill your spot."

Please, Ryan, hold your tongue, I mentally tell him. Thankfully, he seems to get the message. He looks at the floor, clearly not excited to work with Peter.

Tix shows us off the stage and back down the hall. Once the cameras are off him,

Tix goes back to being his grouchy self. "Kids these days," he mutters.

***

That evening, Ryan and I decide to head down to the beach to talk. But neither of us knows what to say, so we walk along the shore in silence. The ocean waves lap at our feet, reflecting the pink sky. The wind coming off the water is cold, and I wish I'd brought my sweatshirt.

Finally I turn to Ryan and blurt out the question that's burning in my mind. "Should we drop out of the competition?"

"What? No way!" he exclaims. "Look how far we've come. We already made it this far— we just have to beat those other seven groups. We can totally do this, Eve."

There's a bit of nervousness in his voice, but his enthusiasm makes me feel better.

"I just wish I could compete alongside you," I say.

"Me too. But remember that as long as one of us wins, we both get the record deal."

We stare out at the water for a moment, and then Ryan sticks out his hand toward me.

"Promise you won't go easy on me," he says.

I grin. Maybe everything will work out. "I promise."

We shake hands and then head back to the studio to get a good night's sleep.

CHAPTER 4

The next day is the first day of practice with my new team. When I arrive in the rehearsal room, a cameraman is setting up his equipment, preparing to film my every move. My teammates file in shortly after me. Two of them are the punk duo I saw yesterday: Delia and Casey. From the instant they arrive, they squabble with each other to get the camera's attention. Our other teammate is Lark, the partner of Asher the cowboy. She sits down and folds her hands in her lap patiently.

Finally, Cassandra drifts into the room. "Good morning, team," she says. Then she explains the plan for the day. Each of us will sing for her to show our strengths and weaknesses. Then she will know how to coach us, to bring each of us to our full potential. She looks at me and says I will be going first.

Cassandra sits in front of me and leans in close to study my mouth as I sing. At the same time, the cameraman shoves the camera way too close to my face. I want to push it away, but instead I clear my throat and sing a scale.

"Give me more power this time," Cassandra says. "Blow me away with your voice. I want to fall backward."

I try again, but she interrupts me before I've done half the scale.

"No, my dear. Not strong enough! Where is your passion? Where is your heart? Put it all in your voice!"

I try again and again. But each time Cassandra shakes her head, crosses her arms, and sighs. A huge wave of disappointment washes over me. My idol chose me, and I'm letting her down. But I don't know what I'm doing wrong. I don't know how to be more passionate. I thought I loved making music, but Cassandra seems to think something's holding me back. I wish Ryan were here to encourage me.

The punk duo, Casey and Delia, take turns after me. They sound like they're yelling instead of singing. But Cassandra doesn't ask where their passion is. She nods at them.

Now it's Lark's turn. Her voice rings out like notes from a piano, from the deepest deep to the highest high. I'm instantly entranced. This girl knows her stuff. It's beautiful and clear—maybe even better than Cassandra's voice. Even the punks' mouths hang open.

"That was gorgeous," Cassandra says when Lark finishes. "Where did you learn to sing?"

"I grew up singing in choir," Lark replies. "So did Asher. We've been partners for years."

"How do you feel about being on a different team than him?"

"It feels . . ." Lark trails off. The camera leans in close to her. Then she says, "Freeing. I feel free to be myself."

She and I make eye contact. I frown, confused as to how she could feel that way. *Good partners should bring out the best in each other*, I think to myself.

***

The next day, Cassandra leads us through writing our own rock song together to perform in the first elimination round. If we win, we get a special advantage for the next round. But if we lose, then one of us is going home. As we work, the punk duo argues over whether we should use the word "heart" or "start" to rhyme with "chart."

Lark moves next to me and together we write our own verses. She looks over my writing and hums to herself. I raise my eyebrows at her, giving her a questioning look. "You're a good singer," she says. "But you need to step out of your comfort zone. That's what Cassandra means by passion."

"Thanks," I murmur. "I didn't really understand her. I was getting a bit frustrated."

"Yeah, this competition is stressful."

She grins at me, looking as beautiful as
her voice.

After a while, the punks manage to scrape
something together. Their lyrics are actually
pretty good. We compare notebooks and
choose the best lines that each of us wrote to
create a final draft of a song. Then we show it
to Cassandra.

She looks over what we have. "Team, I
think we are ready for the first challenge. How
do you feel about singing together as a band, in
front of a live audience?"

The cameras pan over the punks' excited
faces, Lark's small smile, and my nervous
shivering. Then the crew wraps filming.
Tomorrow is the first elimination round.

CHAPTER
5

Tonight, someone is going home. The spotlights dazzle over the stage and the live audience roars as the teams march out from behind the curtain. I smile and wave, but my eyes are on Ryan. I haven't seen him since the beach two days ago. He lifts his hand half-heartedly to the crowd. Dark bags sit under his eyes. Even in the vibrant clothing the producers gave him, he seems deflated. I wonder what horrors he had to endure during his rehearsals.

Then Tix announces that my team is going first. The other teams file onto a small

platform next to the stage containing a row
of chairs so they can watch and cheer us
on—or root for us to lose. I gulp as I tune
my guitar. I just hope we impress the judges.

Cassandra gives us a signal, and then
the spotlights swirl onto me, Lark, Casey,
and Delia.

For a moment, everything is silent but the
hum of the lights and the sound of my breath.
I strum the opening notes, sending out a wave
of energy over the audience. I smile, letting
the music vibrate through me.

Lark sings first, her voice resonating with
my guitar. At the judge's table, Peter, Marina,
and Xavier look pleased. Cassandra remains
motionless and unreadable.

Then Casey and Delia scream into the mics
for the chorus. The mics amplify their voices,
screeching in my ear. Startled, I mess up on
the guitar and lose track of the beat. I try to
recover it but play the wrong chords. It clashes
with the punks' voices.

I freeze up, holding a silent guitar.

When I perform with Ryan, something

like this is an opportunity to improvise on his sampler.

But Casey and Delia aren't Ryan. They turn and glare at me, two identical pairs of raccoon-like eyes.

A soft voice comes out from behind all of us. Lark holds her microphone up to her mouth and finishes singing the punks' verse for them. Suddenly my mistake seems like an intentional pause in the song. I remember what I'm supposed to do. I start playing again, nodding at Lark in thanks.

I sing the final verse. My heart pounds in my ears so I don't hear myself at all. I stare at Cassandra, whose stony face reveals nothing about how I'm doing. I finish singing and the audience erupts into cheers. The judges clap. We walk to the platform where the others are sitting, and the next team comes up to perform.

As I make my way to Ryan, Asher steps out in front of me. "Mighty fine singing voice you have there," he says, grinning a creepy grin and tipping his hat. "I nearly mistook you for a real competitor!"

"Go away, Asher," Lark groans, pushing him aside. "She's not interested in goons like you."

"Aw, don't be like that, little Lark."

She rolls her eyes. "I told you to stop calling me that. I'm both older and taller than you."

I leave them to argue with each other and continue toward Ryan. He gives me a big hug. "Great job!" he says, but I get the sense that he's forcing himself to sound proud. He and I both know I can do much better than this.

Ryan's team goes last. He gives me a wink from the stage. Next to him, Asher does too. I shake my head at Asher, but Ryan sees it and thinks it's for him. He frowns and turns back around before I can do or say anything.

During his performance, all signs of Ryan's exhaustion vanish. The bass throbs and the synthesizers cheer as loud as the crowds. Ryan absorbs all of it into his body and lets it back out. He grooves to the music and even does a split on the stage, surprising everyone including me. The audience cheers. Even Cassandra breaks into a grin. Peter nods his approval.

I squeeze my hands together as I realize, *Ryan doesn't need me to win over a crowd.*

Suddenly, Cassandra's choice to split us up makes sense. She saw how much I shine with Ryan and wants to see me shine just as bright on my own. And Ryan needs to take his own path too.

I look back at the bickering Lark and Asher, the unhappy Casey and Delia, and the rest of the duos among us. *Is this what happens to all duos?* I worry. *They argue, then part ways, and then become two completely different musicians, never to reunite? Because they don't need each other anymore?*

At the end of the round, all the teams line up on the stage while the judges discuss the performances. As I expect, they criticize me for freezing up but praise Lark for thinking fast. I blush, embarrassed at my performance. Ryan gets praised for his awesome dancing and for having fun on the stage.

In the end, the judges choose Ryan's team as the winners of the challenge. Asher claps Ryan hard on the back, making him wince.

Tix marches out to the center of the stage and squints at all of us. "We saw some great performances from all of you tonight, but the time has come to say goodbye to one of our contestants," he says, his voice dropping dramatically. "I will now announce which team will be losing one of its members tonight."

I glance around. Casey and Delia are still glaring at me. With my mistake, I might have made us lose.

But Tix says, "Marina's team, please step forward."

The four contestants on Marina's team gulp loudly and do as they're told. Tix looks intensely at each of them, dragging it out for the sake of suspense. I'm sure the show's editors will add dramatic music later so the viewers at home feel the tension that we all feel now. But right now, no music is needed to capture the mood. I shiver as the contestants shiver, their nervousness washing over me. It could have been me up there.

"Olivia Rooney," Tix says.

One of the girls stiffens.

"You have been eliminated."

Olivia shakes her head in disbelief. Her duo partner, a girl on Ryan's team, runs out to hug her. The cameras follow her off the stage, and then the filming of the first episode is over.

My legs are heavy as I plod back to my room to sleep. In the whirlwind of it all, I don't get the chance to say congratulations to Ryan. I fall asleep as soon as my head hits the pillow.

CHAPTER
6

The next morning, I stumble down to our
practice room in the studio for another day of
hard work. Another day of trying to "find my
passion" or whatever. Another long day where
I don't get to see Ryan at all.

Cassandra starts our lesson by scolding us.
"Last night was not your best work. Obviously,
there was Eve's mistake—"

Casey and Delia shoot me smug grins.

"—but you two lost the soul of the music
as well." She turns to them. "You threw
Eve off when you tried too hard to take the
spotlight. This was a team performance. Your

team is four people, not a duo with some backup singers."

Cassandra claps her hands. "Let's get it together. And stick together."

During vocal training, Cassandra shows Casey and Delia how to hit high notes. How to sing without growling. Lark and I practice adding more strength to our voices. That means getting loud.

When Cassandra takes a break and leaves us alone in the room with the cameras, the punks home in on me.

"We'll show you how to put power into your voice," Delia says. "You're too gentle. This is a competition. Act like it!"

"You want your voice to be like this!" Casey pounds her fist into her palm.

"That's what my guitar is for," I say.

"What if you don't have your guitar?"

"Well, then Ryan—"

"You don't have Ryan now," says Lark.

I fall silent.

"Remember what I said yesterday? About needing to step outside your comfort zone?

I think that means letting go of your duo." I frown at her, not liking the idea of forgetting about Ryan. "It's like Cassandra said. We're not individual members of different duos. We're a band—together. We're here to do new and different things with our music than we ever did before. That will help us all improve."

I realize she's right. I rely on Ryan to fill in when I'm not good enough. He does all the dancing. He makes the beat. I think about all our songs, from "The Quiet Night" to the first one we ever made together when we were eight years old—a silly little tune about how much doing chores sucks. In all of them, my voice is the same: gentle and quiet.

So I should learn how to sing differently, I decide. It will help me write and perform different kinds of songs with Ryan after one of us wins the competition. When we go on tour, we'll be able to take everything we learn here with us.

Casey and Delia nod too. "And we want to learn how to sing more like you two."

"Then let's work together," Lark says. She

sticks her hand out. Casey and Delia put their hands on top of hers. Then I add mine. I grin at the cheesiness of it, and we all laugh.

But even if we're a band, I'm still in a duo with Ryan too, I think. I need to talk to him. I need to tell him what I've been thinking about these past few days. Right when Cassandra comes back, I ask to be excused to the bathroom.

Instead of heading to the bathroom, though, I sneak down the hallway to his team's rehearsal room. I creep along the wall so the cameras can't see me through the doorway. I listen for a moment as Asher sings some kind of country music. Then the coach—Peter— announces it's time to take a break from singing and do some interviews for the viewers of the show. Ryan's going first.

"How come he gets to go first?" Asher complains.

"Because he's better than you," Peter says. "Now, let's go."

There's the sound of shoes shuffling as everyone else clears the room. Asher comes out, his arms crossed and a scowl on his face.

I duck around the corner to hide from the group of them, but thankfully they all go the other way.

I emerge from around the corner, hoping to catch Ryan before the interview. But instead I hear a low grumble of a man's voice—Tix. And then Ryan's voice. But I can't make out the words. I sneak closer to the open door.

"—she wasn't happy for me at all. She seemed kind of bitter that I'd won."

Wait. Is he talking about me? I wonder.

"Usually, people think she's the leader of our duo because she's the vocalist. But you saw how she did last night. She got too nervous and froze up. And I did way better in my performance."

He is *talking about me*, I realize with a sudden burst of sadness.

"So you think she's jealous?" Tix asks.

"She isn't jealous. Eve isn't like that. But maybe she's disappointed. Because she isn't the star of the show for once. I am."

Wow. I slump against the wall. My emotions claw at my insides, leaping from anger to hurt to confusion all in a single second. *Since when has Ryan thought that about me? He has always seemed like the star to me. Why would he say something so mean?*

The only reason I can think of is that he's also realized he doesn't need me to become a star.

I slink back to my own team like a scolded dog. For the rest of the day, my voice stays stuck in my throat. Casey elbows me and asks if I flushed it down the toilet while I was in the bathroom. I give her a half-hearted smile.

That evening, there's a knock on the door to my room. I open it to reveal Ryan in his pajamas. He grins maniacally. "Guess what the reward was for winning yesterday's competition."

I shrug and sit on my bed. "Does it have anything to do with your interview today?"

His face falls. "Huh?"

"I heard what you said about me."

"Oh." He laughs. "I only said that stuff because it adds drama to the show. That's what they're looking for in these interviews.

They don't care about the truth because the truth's boring."

"So you don't actually think that I'm an attention hog?" I blurt out.

"No way," he responds with a shrug.

I stand up, clearly frustrated. "Then why pretend that you do? You made me look like a selfish jerk."

Ryan crosses his arms. "No, I didn't. That's all up to the editing team. If they want you to look like a nice person, trust me—you will. My interview will either make *me* look like a jerk, or that part won't go on TV at all."

"That doesn't make it okay, Ryan! You really hurt my feelings."

He frowns at my anger. "It's just a game, Eve. We have to play it by their rules to win. Don't you want us to win?"

I look away from him. Ryan scuffs his shoe against the carpet for a moment, and then leaves my room with a quiet, "Goodnight."

CHAPTER 7

The next morning, I jump out of bed, throw on my clothes, and run to the studio. Tomorrow is the second elimination round, and someone else is going home. I'm not going to let it be me: I deserve to stay, no matter what anyone, including Ryan, has to say about me.

At the studio, Cassandra calls us into a huddle. "All right, crew. Tomorrow's challenge is going to be a little interesting. Peter's team won last time, and their reward was the chance to assign songs to all the other teams to perform during the challenge. This is our song." She presses play on the speakers.

A happy, jumpy beat starts to play. Then comes a high-pitched female vocalist whose joy is so sickly-sweet I can practically taste sugar. Casey and Delia pretend to gag. Lark's eye twitches. And I glare at the speakers. This is exactly the annoying, cutesy pop I refuse to listen to. And Ryan knows it.

Oh, it's on.

***

Delia smooths out her frilly lace skirt for the hundredth time. "I hate this."

"Me too," Casey moans, tugging at the sparkly ribbons in her jet-black hair.

"We have to play to win," I tell them, even as I glare at the huge red heart printed on my neon pink dress.

It's the night of the second elimination round, and the four of us are waiting to go onstage from behind the curtain. If we can't sing the song well, then we'll at least catch the judges' eyes with our over-the-top popstar attire. I had Blair help us pick out the most ridiculous outfits she could find on the dressing room racks.

Then Tix announces our names, and we bound out to the cheers and laughter of the audience. The annoying pop music starts to play through the speakers over our heads. Behind us, the other contestants laugh at our outfits. Ryan's jaw drops. But I don't care what he thinks because I'm about to give it my all.

I sing my heart out, making my voice higher than it normally is to capture the spirit of the song. Lark also sings well for her part. Casey and Delia, however, struggle to hit the notes. They barely move, too embarrassed by their skirts and ribbons. The judges aren't impressed.

Afterward, Ryan runs up to me on the catwalk, beaming. "Good job!" he exclaims.

"Yeah, I know," I reply curtly.

He looks confused.

After every team has performed, Tix comes on the stage to announce the results. Since Ryan's team had the advantage of picking songs, they go on to win for the second time in a row. And unfortunately, my team did the worst. He calls all of us forward. And just like that, Delia gets sent home.

CHAPTER

8

"You could have done something." Casey glowers at me and Lark during practice the next morning. "You could have talked to Ryan or Asher—asked them to give us an easier song. You could have saved Delia."

The cameras zoom in on our faces to catch our reactions. With Cassandra currently out of the room, I decide to roll my eyes. "The competition doesn't work that way," I say. "Ryan and I are on different teams now—I couldn't ask him to do something like that even if I wanted to, and you know it. And besides, Ryan and I made a promise we wouldn't go easy on each other."

"Asher said he'd only help me if he gets something out of it too," Lark says.

"Some friends you are," Casey mutters, sniffling. Her makeup is a bit runny today.

With that, whatever sense of being a band we had before is gone. Casey spends the next few team practices getting in our way. She butts in and sings over me and Lark. She stands in front of us when we rehearse performances. She demands Cassandra make her the lead vocalist, muttering that she's *clearly* the most passionate of us all.

Passionate or not, she doesn't sync up with me and Lark at all. We go through another three elimination rounds, and our band always falls in second or third place. During the performances, Lark and I harmonize and play off each other's voices. But Casey yells into the microphone and slams her bass. It's a clashing wreck. Even Cassandra winces. Every round, we're inches away from another of us getting sent home.

On top of that, there's nothing we can do

to beat Ryan's team. With their incredible voices and dynamic dancing, they sweep the audience off their feet and win challenge after challenge.

After every elimination round, the producers interview each of the remaining competitors. In his interviews, Ryan brags about how much better than me he is. He lists off the instruments he can play, and when he shifts to me he claims I only play the guitar, ignoring that I sing too. In another interview, he points out it was his idea to audition for *The Right Note*. I'm sure the editors show this clip with the moment where Cassandra told me to be more passionate, so I end up looking like I don't care as much as Ryan does. When Tix asks if Ryan wants me to get eliminated, Ryan shrugs and says, "I'm here to win. If I have to beat Eve, I will."

In my own interviews, when the producers push me to criticize Ryan, I just tell them I want to talk about my own singing. "I've improved a lot since coming onto the show," I say. "I'm really proud of that."

With these interviews and the elimination rounds happening every three days and no time to rest in between because of vocal training and rehearsals, I feel myself burning out. I drag myself out of bed every morning and perform on autopilot. My excitement at getting closer to the final stages of the competition isn't enough to counter the feeling that Ryan wants to see me lose. And with how well his team is doing, he just might get his wish granted.

Then, during their next performance, Ryan's team finally messes up. As he dances, Ryan trips over Asher's foot and crashes into another boy in their band. They both tumble across the stage, and the audience lets out a collective, "Ooh." Ryan gets up immediately, but for the rest of the song his voice is shaky and flat. The other boy, mortified, can't even let out a single note. The judges aren't impressed. They give my team the win for the first time, and the boy from Ryan's band is the sixth competitor to be eliminated.

As we head backstage, I overhear Ryan

whisper angrily to Asher, "You tripped me on purpose."

Asher laughs. "What are you gonna do about it?"

"We're supposed to be a team," Ryan protests, but Asher has already started walking away. I feel a surge of relief. Their team isn't perfect after all.

I tell Lark what I saw, and she doesn't look surprised. "Asher's very competitive," she says. "It sounds like he's jealous of Ryan."

Out of the corner of my eye is a flash of blond hair. Blair appears with a cameraman by her side. She pulls me aside and asks if I can give a quick interview. "Just one question this time," she says.

All I want to do is go to bed, but I remember Ryan saying we have to play by the show's rules if we want to win. "All right," I say.

Blair nods. "Ryan has been saying he's here to win. He wants to out-sing you. Do you think that's possible?"

I blink at her, not really knowing what to say. *Out-sing me?* I think to myself. *Did he really say that? I can't believe it.*

Blair senses my hesitation and presses me for an answer. "Which of you is the better singer?"

I think back to what Ryan said—this is all just a game. It's all about keeping people interested and winning over the judges. If the show wants a conflict, then I'll give them one. "I am," I say, even if I don't really believe it. "I'm the vocalist in our duo for a reason."

"Ouch," says Blair as she grins wickedly. I can tell this is exactly what she was looking for, and instantly I regret my words. But it's already been recorded. It's going to show up on TV, and everyone's going to think it's real.

***

Now that six of the competitors have been eliminated and only ten of us remain, the judges split up the teams. Moving forward, we will all perform as solo acts so the judges can assess our individual skills. We'll still get to work with the same coach and continue with the eliminations as usual, but now only one contestant will win each challenge. We'll compete until only four of us remain.

For the first solo challenge, we're told to choose a slip of paper containing a song title from a hat. While there are ten of us, there are only five song options—meaning each song will be performed by two people. It's sort of a twisted version of duos, where now each pair of us must try to outshine each other. The song I pick is one I know well. Ryan's face turns pale as he stares at his slip of paper. I see the title of his song . . . it's the same as mine.

During the challenge, I perform to the best of my ability, hitting all the long notes and showing off my range. Ryan is less successful. His voice cracks when he goes high, and he doesn't hit the right notes when he goes low. But he acts out the lyrics on stage like a play. He drops to one knee, pulls his fist to his chest dramatically. The audience loves it. They cheer loud—louder than they did for me.

Although neither of us win, we both make it through to the next round along with seven other contestants. The judges praise my singing and Ryan's dancing, which gets on my nerves. "This is a singing competition," I say in an interview after the performances. "Not a dance competition."

As I exit the studio, I catch a glimpse of Ryan doing his own interview. "I can sing too," he says, looking into the camera. "I'm not just a backup musician in our duo. I can do everything Eve can do and more."

My stomach drops. *I don't think Ryan is a backup musician at all! We're a duo. Partners. Right?* I try telling myself he doesn't really believe these things, but he looks so serious when he says it.

I cross my arms and think about what I've said to the cameras. The producers have been pushing us to compete with each other, instead of against the other duos, so maybe it's all their fault that this is happening. But Ryan has also said some hurtful things without the producers asking him to. He started this whole mess.

Ryan continues, "Eve should be really worried about me as a competitor. The audience loves me way more than her. They always have."

I clench my fists so hard my nails leave marks in my palms.

The next day, I practically waltz into the practice room. Lark stares at me as I spin on my toes and swoop my arms out like a ballerina.

"I know what each of us has to do to win," I tell her. "Come dance with me."

Grinning, she takes my hand.

I look at Casey, who sits across the room, wearing her earbuds so she doesn't have to talk to us. I walk over to her and tap her on the shoulder.

She plucks out one of her earbuds. "What do you want?"

"Can you play that song through the speakers?" I ask.

She stares at me with wide, surprised eyes.

"And teach us how to dance to it," I add.

She bursts into laughter. But then she plugs her phone into Cassandra's speakers. Angry guitars blast through the room. Then Casey grabs me and Lark and shows us how to stomp our feet, shake our heads, and bob our bodies to the beat. After a while, I pick out the parts of the song where I should wave my hands or head bang. The song starts to sound less like noise and more like music.

When Cassandra arrives, she sees all of us stomping around like maniacs. But instead of stopping us, she joins in.

By the next elimination round, we're ready to rock. For this challenge, we have to coordinate original choreography with a song of our choice. The three of us all picked loud rock songs to show off our new moves. Lark performs first, then Casey, and then me. We each dance around the stage with an electrifying energy. I can tell the judges are impressed with our passion—they're smiling more and dancing along through our performances.

At the end of my song, I let out a roar into the mic: a big scream, like Casey and Delia taught me how to do. The crowd goes wild.

I'm still panting when the rest of the contestants join me on the stage. This time, I win the challenge, with Casey and Lark in second and third places!

Cassandra beams at me from her spot at the table, glowing with pride. "As the winner of tonight's round, you've earned *immunity* for the next round! That means you're safe from elimination."

Whoa, I think. That brings me ahead of the other seven competitors and closer than ever to the record deal prize.

"In addition," Xavier continues, "you get to pick one other contestant to also get immunity. Who would you like to save from the chance of elimination?" He extends a hand toward my competitors lined up next to me.

Tix hands me his microphone.

I turn and look at the other contestants. Casey crosses her arms. Asher winks. Ryan stands with his hands behind his back, looking weary. *So much for the audience liking him better, huh?* I think. Lark has her hands in her pockets and wears a small smile.

"I choose Lark," I say into the mic.

As she comes up and gives me a hug, I catch Ryan's eye. I expect him to be angry or frustrated, but he just looks sad.

CHAPTER

9

That night, I only get a little sleep. When I do manage to doze off, I have a nightmare about being on stage. Ryan sits at the judge's table, with two buttons in front of him: one for yes, and one for no. Tix's voice asks, "What do you choose, Ryan? Do you want Eve on your team?" I wake up right before Ryan makes his choice.

Guilt washes over me as I lie in the dark. *I should have picked Ryan to share immunity with me*, I think. But then another voice in my head pipes up, *He abandoned you!* I spend the rest of the night arguing with myself.

At 7:00 a.m., I trudge sleepily into the rehearsal room where Cassandra explains the next challenge. All the contestants have to perform a song from a musical. All of them except for me and Lark, that is, because we both have immunity. Instead we get to watch the challenge from the audience.

"Lucky," Casey grumbles at us. "I hate musicals!"

***

While I'm waiting backstage on the night of the challenge, Lark rushes over to me. "Can I talk to you?" she whispers.

"Um, sure."

She takes my hand and we exit to the hallway. Stagehands and camera crews charge past us. Lark ushers me to some vending machines in the corner.

"What's up?" I ask.

Lark glances over her shoulder. "Eve, I'm worried about you," she says. "You seem really stressed out."

I sigh. I hadn't realized it was so obvious,

but we've been spending a lot of time together lately so I can't say I'm surprised that she's noticed. "Yeah, I guess I kind of am."

"From my point of view, it looks like Ryan's the one causing all your stress. He keeps saying these mean things about you. He's throwing you under the bus for the sake of stardom."

"That's true, but . . . he's still my friend," I say.

"He isn't really acting like your friend," Lark says.

I look down at my feet.

"I'm sorry, Eve. I'm only saying this because I care about you. We've become good friends, haven't we? I think we could make good partners after *The Right Note* is all over. What do you think?"

I frown. "You mean, like, we become a duo?"

"Yeah." She smiles, her eyes bright. "If I win the final round, I'll let you join my band and record an album with me. And if you win, I can join yours. We could go on tour together. We could be famous."

I think back to my dream of Ryan choosing between the yes and no buttons.

"I'm sorry, Lark," I say. "But I'm in a duo with Ryan. I can't turn my back on him."

She lets out a sigh. "Okay. But if you change your mind, let me know."

We return backstage. Tix's voice sounds from the other side of the curtain. As he announces the contestants' names, we all head out into the bright lights.

CHAPTER 10

Casey goes home after the musical challenge. Her punk attitude and singing style has gotten a bit repetitive for the judges. She holds her head up high as the audience gives her a final cheer.

The next round had us singing without any music accompaniment. I expected Ryan to be too nervous to sing well. But during the challenge, he belted his heart out. He's gotten a lot better at hitting the notes.

After that challenge, the remaining six contestants return backstage to wait for Blair to come interview each of us. In the darkness, I scan the rest of the group for Lark. Ryan

is in the farthest corner away from me,
listening to music on his phone. The other two
competitors set up a card game on the floor.
Asher munches on a bag of popcorn. He sees
me looking at him and comes over to offer
me some.

"No thanks," I say.

"Just thought you could use some cheering
up." He throws a couple pieces into his mouth.
"Figured you'd be devastated by the news."

"What news?"

"You know, about Ryan."

I look over at Ryan. "What are you talking
about? What happened?"

"Aw, you really don't know?" Asher grins
triumphantly. "He and I are gonna be a music
duo. He asked me yesterday to join him in a
new band, just the two of us."

"Just the two of you . . . ?" I repeat.

"That's right. We decided to put aside
our differences and work together to take
you down."

I peer at Asher, trying to find the joke in
his face. Because this has to be a joke. But his

expression is earnest. My stomach sinks.

"No way. It couldn't . . . how could he?" I stutter. I shove past Asher and rush over to Ryan. "Ryan, did you—"

But before I can finish my question, Ryan catches my eye, turns the volume all the way up on his music, and heads for the door. He doesn't even acknowledge that I'd been trying to talk to him.

"I really am sorry about this, Eve," Asher says, suddenly sympathetic. "I didn't want to take your spot in the duo from you, but Ryan insisted. And you know how great of a musician he is. How could I say no?"

My voice gets caught in my throat. *How can this be happening? How can this be real?* Tears form in my eyes.

"Here. Have some popcorn." Asher grins and holds out the bag again. "It's the least I can do."

I burst out of the backstage area and rush through the studio, charging down hallways and opening doors until I'm out of breath and tears. I push past cameramen, stagehands, and even Tix. "Watch where you're going!" he yells after me.

I nearly bowl over Blair. She flattens herself against the wall as I sprint past her. "If you're looking for Ryan, he went that way," she says, pointing to the left.

I turn right instead. I yank open the door to the girl's bathroom near the dressing room. There, I find Lark washing her hands.

"Oh, hi, Eve," she starts, but then she sees that I'm crying.

We stare at each other while I catch my breath and try to find my voice.

"I changed my mind, Lark," I finally wheeze. "Let's form a duo."

CHAPTER
11

At our next practice, Lark is chipper like
a songbird. She tries to cheer me up by
complimenting my voice. Even though we
are competing as individuals, she suggests
we sing a duet to practice our harmonizing,
which is something I've never done with Ryan
before. Our voices meld together beautifully.
Cassandra walks in on us practicing and claps,
her face full of delight. But even with the joy
of singing alongside a friend—and partner—
again, I feel like something's missing. When
we finish our song, I take a break and head to
the bathroom to clear my mind.

My face in the mirror is paler than usual. My eyes are a flat gray, not their usual blue. I take a few deep breaths and sigh.

I splash my face with some water before leaving the bathroom. As soon as I turn down the hall to the rehearsal room, Asher and Ryan appear at the opposite end of the hallway. Ryan's frustration is obvious even from fifty feet away. He jerks his hands around as he speaks to Asher, who just smiles, shrugs, and rolls his eyes. This only makes Ryan angrier. I hurry to get back to the room before they reach me.

As soon as I touch the doorknob, I overhear Asher say, "Go ask her yourself if you don't believe me." He gestures toward me.

Oh no.

Ryan stomps over to me.

"Is it true? You're starting a duo with Lark?" he hisses.

I want to retort, *And* you're *starting a duo with Asher!* But instead I keep my cool. "Yes, I am."

He clenches his fists. "Then I'm going to send both of you home. You and Lark."

"Fine. I'll be waiting." I cross my arms.

Asher interrupts our stare down. "Come on, Ryan," he says. "Let's go get ready for the challenge."

Anxiety swells in my chest for the next hour as I rehearse. My voice falls flat and hits the wrong notes. From her chair, Lark urges me to sing stronger. My heart pounds too hard, and my hands and knees shake from stress. My voice catches in my throat and comes out like a gargle. I cough a few times and start again, but it's still no better.

"Maybe you should take a break," Lark suggests, gesturing to a seat.

"Good idea," says Cassandra. "Let your voice rest for a bit."

Suddenly, Cassandra's phone buzzes in her pocket. She pulls it out and answers, nodding as she listens. Then her eyes widen. "Oh, I see," she says. "Yes, well, that's fine with me. It's certainly interesting. Yes. All right. Thanks for letting me know. I'll pass on the good news."

"What's going on?" I ask when she hangs up.

Cassandra smiles. "Tomorrow's challenge has been called off."

"Called off?" Lark repeats.

"What do you mean?" I frown.

"Two of the other contestants have decided to nominate themselves for a sing-off," Cassandra explains. "Whoever loses will be going home."

"Which two contestants?" I narrow my eyes.

Cassandra says the names I least expect. "It'll be Asher versus Ryan."

I make eye contact with Lark, hoping she knows something I don't. Her brow furrows with worry, and her small mouth twists into a frown. She's just as confused as I am.

"What's with the long faces?" Cassandra puts her hands on her hips. "Cheer up! This means you two are automatically one step closer to the final four."

All I can feel is dread creeping through my veins.

Then, without a word, Lark jumps to her feet and rushes to the door.

"Wait, Lark—" I start, but before I can

stop her, she pushes past Cassandra and sprints down the hall. I stumble out after her, but she rounds the corner and disappears. *Where is she going?* I wonder.

Hoping Lark will return, Cassandra and I go back to trying to get my voice to work but to no avail. And when Lark doesn't show up, I get more and more worried, which just makes me sound even worse.

The only thing I can think of is that Lark went to talk to Asher. *Does she secretly want him to stay? Even after we talked about working together?* Cassandra pats me on the shoulder, but it doesn't help. I sweat and shake, as if I'm the one going on stage for elimination. I decide I need to talk to Ryan. I'm tired of hearing things from everyone else—I need to hear them from him. I need to know what's going on.

***

The night of the elimination round, Asher and Ryan are already both backstage preparing for their sing-off. They stand on opposite sides of the room, Asher lounging about like a happy cat and Ryan fuming like a wild bull. Asher gives me a wave as I enter the room, but Ryan just puts his headphones on and taps at his sampler in angry silence.

Swallowing the lump in my throat, I walk over to Ryan. He ignores me until I press the off button on the corner of the sampler.

He yanks the headphones off his ears. "What do you want?"

"I want to know what's going on here," I tell him, keeping my voice low so Asher doesn't overhear. "What on earth are you thinking? A sing-off?"

"What, you don't think I can beat Asher?"

"No, that's not what I mean." I pinch the bridge of my nose. "I just don't get why you chose to challenge him."

"Seriously?" Ryan scoffs. "He's been trying to get me eliminated all season. You saw how he tripped me a few challenges back. He's jealous of me. It didn't bother me until he told me about your pact with Lark. When I got upset, he just made fun of me. That was the final straw." Ryan huffs. "Someone like that doesn't deserve to win *The Right Note*. So I challenged him to a sudden death match. Loser goes home—no shot at the grand prize."

I turn and look back at Asher. He smirks at me.

"So . . . you and Asher aren't forming a duo?" I ask Ryan.

"Of course not!"

"But I thought . . ." I stare past Ryan. "He lied to me."

"What?" Ryan looks at me, confused. "Who are you talking about?"

"Asher told me that you asked him to be in a band with him after the show." Tears burn in my eyes. "And I believed him. I thought you were screwing me over. I was so mad at you. So I told Lark I would make a band with her to get back at you. To prove I didn't need you, just like you didn't need me."

Ryan's mouth opens, but nothing comes out. Through my blurry vision, I study his shocked face. His slouching posture. His hair, which has faded from blue to gray. I realize

I haven't seen him smile in days. All because of Asher.

I whirl on my heel, my hair and jacket whipping in the air. "You tricked me," I yell at Asher. "You made me betray my friend."

Asher takes one look at me and his smile completely melts away. I stomp toward him and he backs up, holding up his hands to calm me down. But his eyes are full of fear. And I am full of rage.

"Wait a second," he says. "Just hold on now."

I don't wait a second or hold on. I keep marching at him.

Asher trips over a pile of wires and ropes and lands on the floor. He crawls backward over the floor. "It was just part of the show! It's a competition! I was just—"

I stand over him, furious.

"Stop!" Lark's voice rings out across the room.

Everyone freezes. We turn and look to see her standing in the doorway.

"Eve, wait," she says. "It isn't Asher's fault."

"Yes, it is. He lied to me. To us." I gesture to Ryan.

"No, he—well, okay. Yes, he did. But it wasn't his idea."

"Then whose was it?" Ryan demands.

Lark takes a deep breath. She looks right at me, lips pursed, guilt and shame making her cheeks turn red.

"You?" I say in disbelief.

She lets out a huge sigh. "Hear me out, okay?" she says. "I care about you, Eve. I saw how Ryan was being a bad friend to you. I had to do something to help you. I wanted you to realize that Ryan isn't the best partner for you."

A lump forms in my throat.

"I am." She pats herself on the chest. "When you turned my offer down, I had to do something to help you realize. So I asked Asher to lie to you for me. Because I couldn't do it to your face. I couldn't hurt you like that."

"You have hurt me, though." My throat clenches as I push down tears.

"I know. I'm sorry. But I did it for you, Eve."

I shake my head. "I can't be in a duo with someone who lies to me. The deal's off, Lark."

Lark slumps.

I turn away from her and look back down at Asher. "See?" he says. "It wasn't my idea."

"But you didn't have to help Lark." I cross my arms.

"And miss an opportunity to drive a wedge between you and Ryan? No way." He stands up and brushes off his jeans. All his smug confidence has returned to him. "And it worked, too, because I'm about to send Ryan home. After him, you're next, Eve." He pushes past me and disappears behind the curtain.

Ryan and I look at each other. There's still sadness and confusion in his expression, but when he sees me his eyes light up again. I take a deep breath. This might be his last time performing.

"Ryan," I say. "I know you might not think I'm telling the truth, but I believe in you. Good luck."

He smiles. "Thanks, Eve."

CHAPTER

12

Asher sings first. The winks and smiles he throws to the crowds of screaming teenage girls are a huge hit. His voice, impressively deep and smooth, waves over the audience. He reaches down and grabs the hands of a few fans as he sings, basking in the attention. His voice sounds perfect as he hits every note, but there is something missing. Asher has no love for singing, only a desire to win, and it shows in his performance.

After a hearty round of applause, Asher returns to his seat. Then he bumps shoulders with Ryan and sneers, "Nice knowing you."

"Certainly was," Ryan sing-songs in reply. He bows dramatically, then runs down to the stage. I grin. *This is the Ryan I'm used to*, I think.

In the moment before the song starts, silence rules over the stage. Ryan adjusts his stance and stretches his fingers over his sampler's keyboard. I see him take a breath. Then the speakers spark to life.

Ryan's voice starts off a little shaky, but by the next verse he belts out the notes without a single mistake. Unlike Asher's version of the song, Ryan's is full of passion. He adds flourish by singing runs of notes while slamming the keys. He stomps in rhythm with the beat and swings his arms as he hits the harder notes.

At the end of the song, the instrumentals die off, and Ryan is left to sing the final lines by himself. He settles in the center of the stage, pulls the microphone close to his mouth, and holds the last note. As it echoes through the theater, he reaches into his pocket and hurls a fistful of glitter into the air.

Everyone gasps. The glitter sparkles like stars. Ryan closes his eyes and lets it fall onto him. The applause that follows is deafening. The judges even stand up as they clap. Peter, Ryan's vocal trainer, beams with pride.

"What an *out of this world* performance!" Tix cries. "From a musician who was once scared to sing to a true artist. This is the kind of transformation made possible by *The Right Note*."

I lean back in my seat, letting Tix's words soak in. Ryan really *has* come a long way. Whether motivated by the risk of elimination or the emotional roller coaster before the show, he sang like he never has before.

The judges call Asher back down from his seat. Their decision is swift and easy. Ryan outshines Asher by a long shot. Asher gapes with shock when they tell him he's the one going home. He casts one final glance up at me and Lark, and then descends from the stage.

***

That evening, Ryan and I walk along the ocean shore at sunset just like we did a month ago. It's colder tonight, and not even dog walkers join us. Only the gulls and the waves are here.

Things are still tense between us, but we both want to make it better. Ryan lets me talk first. "After you said those things about me, I wanted you to apologize," I say. "You said you were just 'playing the game,' but I didn't get why you couldn't play the game differently."

Ryan stares out at the water. I can tell he's not happy with what I said, but he's not denying it either. I take a deep breath and continue, "And then, things got . . . I don't know. We started competing against each other for real. Trying to get rid of each other instead of trying to help each other."

"I felt like you were abandoning me for Lark," Ryan says. "I wanted to do whatever it took to stay in the running. I had to get better at singing, or else I was worried you'd choose her instead of me."

I laugh. "Seeing you get better at singing made me worry you'd want to become a solo artist." I nudge his elbow with mine. "And then what would you need me for?"

"No one else has your voice, Eve."

"And no one else can be my best friend, Ryan," I say, smiling at him.

"I'm sorry."

"I'm sorry too." Ryan and I hug, and just like that everything is forgiven. We're a duo, after all.

CHAPTER 13

Our final week in California flies by faster
than a pop song. After Asher's elimination,
one of the other guys from his and Ryan's
band gets eliminated in the next round. Ryan
and I grab each other's arms and jump together
in celebration. We're the only duo to survive
to the final four. Just like that, it's time for the
final performance where the judges choose
a winner.

"It's time to prepare for the final round!"
Tix tells us. "You have twenty-four hours."

As the camera crews begin to wrap up,
I pull Lark aside. I tell her that while I don't

like that she lied to me, I understand that she thought she was helping me and I forgive her. She just gives me a sad smile.

Cassandra and I train one-on-one the next morning. She leans in close, and the camera leans in even closer. I don't even blink. "Let's hear that scale," she instructs.

I go through the motions.

"That's the best you can do?" She winks.

I grin mischievously. "You might want to back up," I tell the cameraman. He raises his eyebrows like he doesn't believe me but takes a step back.

I take a deep breath and sing. I put all my love for music into my voice. The notes flow out of me like a river, flooding the room and washing over Cassandra.

"Wow," she says when I finish the scale. "You've found your passion, Eve."

"Really?"

Cassandra nods. "All season you've been getting better and stronger. I could feel the stress and anger in your voice. Those emotions motivated you to improve, but you still couldn't break free. What you needed was love and peace. Where did you find it?"

I think back to my first session with Cassandra, when I couldn't blow her away with my voice. "Ryan," I tell her. "Being with him drives me to be the best musician I can."

Cassandra folds her hands in her lap. "At first I thought you were relying on him too much. But I understand now it wasn't reliance but connection. Music should bring people together out of joy and love."

"Thanks for everything, Cassandra," I say.

As I exit the room, I pass by Lark. I wish her good luck. But she's never had any trouble finding her own passion. She'll blow Cassandra away on the first try.

***

When I round the corner and make it back out to the lobby of the studio, I get a huge surprise: my parents! I sprint into their arms, only now realizing how much I miss them. They explain that they flew out to watch me perform in the final four.

"Ryan's parents are here too," my mom says. "We'll sit next to them and cheer you both on."

Just like back home. The thought of my parents screaming like teenagers in the crowd makes me laugh and calms my nerves. But then I remember they've never seen me perform without Ryan by my side. I wonder how much of our conflict will make it into the final cut of the show.

Then I get an idea. If Ryan and Asher could bend the rules with a sudden death sing-off, maybe I can too. I tell my parents I have to go back to rehearsal and escape into the depths of the studio, hunting for the white-blond, chattery head of Blair.

***

Rainbow lights bloom over the stage like sunflowers, illuminating the theater with every color imaginable. Theme music blasts over the speakers as the cameras swoop down from the ceiling, getting shots of the screaming audience and the stern judges. Then a camera drops down over the stage and sweeps across from left to right, capturing the faces of the final four contestants: Lark, Jasper, Ryan, and me.

Tix comes out from the side of the stage. He wears his trademark glittery suit, which shines almost as much as his bald head.

"Welcome, everyone!" he cries. "Welcome to the final episode of this season of *The Right Note*. This past month, we've seen sixteen talented teens compete for these final four spots. The victors stand before you tonight. We have the duo who made it to the end, Eve Hardt and Ryan Okri! The underdog who made a huge comeback, Jasper Ishikawa! And, last but not least, Lark Pelletier!

"These four will be competing for the grand prize—a record deal with Wild Hill Studio. Who will be the next winner of *The Right Note*? Let's find out!"

The audience goes nuts. I spy my parents waving at me from the front row, just to the right of the judges' table. My heart swells.

Lark will be singing first. Jasper, Ryan,

and I climb to our seats to watch her. She readies herself in the center of the stage, carrying an acoustic guitar.

The background noise of the audience dies down. She takes a huge breath. Then she strums a few chords on the guitar. I recognize the song at once: it's the same one Cassandra performed during her own final round. A winner's song.

Lark opens her mouth. The music that comes out of her sounds as naturally beautiful as birdsong. The spotlights move slowly. Calm fills the theater, as if everyone is holding their breath.

After the first few verses, she plays the guitar faster and louder and sings harder to match it. She stares directly into the camera, her eyes burning intensely. Her voice quivers with emotion. The final note fills the room.

Then she drops her head, closes her mouth, and quiets the guitar. Entranced with the magic of her performance, it takes a few seconds for the audience to react. Their applause rolls over her like thunder. She looks up, as if awakening from a long slumber. She bows gracefully. At the judges' table, Cassandra wipes her eyes.

Next up is Jasper. As he rocks out his rendition of an Elvis Presley song, I lean over to Lark and congratulate her on her own performance. She shrugs, fighting back a smile.

Ryan taps the railing of the catwalk to the beat of Jasper's song. I nudge him, and he jolts. "You ready to rock?" I ask him.

"More than ready," he grins back.

Jasper finishes, and his chest heaves as he catches his breath and wipes the sweat from his forehead. The judges clap.

It's time to take to the stage for my final performance. I start down the stairs, Ryan on my heels. His hand rests on my shoulder in reassurance.

Tix walks out to the center of the stage. "As you all know," he says. "This season of *The Right Note* had a special theme of 'teamwork.' We took duos from all over the country, split them up, and pitted them against each other. Tonight, we're going to bring one of those duos back together. Two of the final four contestants will compete as one."

The audience hushes in anticipation of the announcement.

"Please welcome Eve and Ryan to the stage!"

We race out to the cheers of the crowds. I lift my guitar over my head in response. When the applause finally dies down and Tix steps out of the view of the cameras, we begin.

The performance starts with my soft, clear voice. I look right into the camera centered over the judges' heads, which eyes us like a fifth judge. Ryan plays long chords on his sampler to underscore my voice. The sound builds and builds until it's ready to break.

I launch into playing loud, rocking guitar. Ryan pounds at his sampler in response to me, playing notes that flow with the sound. The strings of my guitar vibrate in tune with my voice, then Ryan's. Our different styles step into sync.

Then we do something we've never done before. I lean in close to the microphone. Ryan leans in too. Inches away from each other, we harmonize the final verses as a duet.

Our music cascades over the audience. They raise their hands and call out in time with us. I grin at Ryan, and he grins at me. Our love for music makes us shine bright. We don't need a record deal with Wild Hill Studio to share that love with people. And we don't need a reality TV show to tell us how to really play our music. We truly are the best partners for each other.

When our final performance comes to an end, I give Ryan a huge hug. The audience's applause is deafening. Tix returns to the stage to banish us to the catwalk, where all four of the contestants have to wait for the judges to decide on the winner.

My heart pounds as I ascend the stairs. Every sound in the room echoes in my ears. I hear the judges whispering and scratching their papers with their pens. I hear the murmuring of the audience. The whirring of the cameras. The heartbeats of Ryan, Lark, and Jasper as we await the judges' decision.

After what feels like an entire lifetime, Tix calls us all back down. We line up against the curtain again.

I squeeze Ryan's hand.

Tix spreads his arms.

"And the winner of *The Right Note* is . . ."

CHAPTER 14

"Lark Pelletierrrrr!"

Lark falls to her knees, her eyes wide in shock. The judges embrace her as shimmering confetti shoots out of cannons on either side of the stage. Color and light swirl around us. Ryan turns to me and I hug him. The last footage of *The Right Note* concludes with a shot of all of us—the contestants, judges, and Tix—on the stage surrounded by the sparkling bits of paper.

Once we get outside of the studio, my parents express their frustration with the results. "It should have been you! What are they thinking?" my mom grumbles.

"It's okay," I say, patting them on their shoulders. "I'm ready to go home."

They climb into a taxi with all my luggage and head to the airport. I'll join them shortly for the trip home. But first I say my goodbyes to Blair, who hugs me with tears in her eyes. Then Cassandra, who tells me she can't wait to listen to the first album Ryan and I put out there. And finally, Lark. I find her on the steps leading up to the back door of the studio, staring at the certificate declaring her the winner of *The Right Note*.

"What are you doing out here?" I ask, startling her.

She folds the certificate in half. "Avoiding the reporters. They all want to interview me."

"Don't you want to be on TV?"

She snorts.

I sit down next to her. "Congratulations, by the way. You deserve it."

"We all deserved it," she says. "You especially, Eve. You're one of the coolest people I've ever met. You could stay here in California. We could make an album together."

"I appreciate the offer, Lark, but I think I need to take a break from all of this for a while." I touch her shoulder as I get up. "I'll keep my eye out for your name on the charts."

Out in front of the building, I meet up with Ryan. The taxi pulls up moments later and we take off, leaving the giant glass studio behind.

***

A knock sounds at the front door. I groan, drop my biology textbook onto my bed, and then head downstairs to tell yet another reporter that I'm done giving interviews. Ever since I got back from California, reporter after reporter has wanted to talk to me about the show. I've had enough of TV and being forced into a false reality just to drive up ratings. They all ask the same questions: "What was it like being on the stage? What was your judge Cassandra like in person? What about Tix?"

Sometimes they ask about me about Ryan, "What was it like having to compete against him? Are you two in a band again?" But the worst one is, "Is he your boyfriend?" I shut the door in their face if they ask me that.

The truth is, I haven't seen much of Ryan since we've gotten home. With all the make-up work for school I have to do, there hasn't been any time to play music. I hum to myself quietly as I study—not even my parents hear me.

As I turn the doorknob, I prepare to tell whatever reporter is waiting outside to get lost.

But it isn't a reporter standing on my front steps. It's Ryan.

He runs a hand through his now-pink hair nervously. "Hey. Is this a bad time?"

I shake my head and relax into a smile. "No, I was just studying. What's up?"

He reaches into his back pocket and pulls out a crumpled envelope. "Guess what this is."

"Your report card?" I ask, jokingly.

"It's an invitation to play at the city arts festival this summer." Ryan breaks into a huge grin. "They want us to headline the concert. As a duo. What do you say?"

"We'd have to start getting ready now," I say, observing the date written on the invitation. It's only one month away. "I don't know, Ryan. I still have a ton of homework."

"Me too. But I can't stand it anymore. I have to sing or I'll lose my mind. Don't you feel that way too?"

"Maybe a little bit."

"Also," he says, unfolding the letter. He points at a line of text on the paper. "It's totally *unplugged*. That means no electronics allowed. No phones, no electric instruments—"

"No cameras," I muse.

"It'd be just us and the stage."

I glance over my shoulder, thinking about all the homework still waiting for me. With a mischievous smile I reply, "Okay. Just one song."

ABOUT THE AUTHOR

D. A. Graham divides his time between writing and wishing he was writing. He lives in Minneapolis, Minnesota, with his boyfriend and an assortment of foster cats.

Escape!

The Island

THE ONE

The Right Note

Treasure Hunt

Warrior Zone

MASON FALLS MYSTERIES

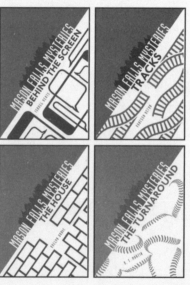

EVEN AN ORDINARY TOWN
HAS ITS SECRETS.